Where I Live

For Eliza

Where I Live

Christopher Wormell

Dial Books for Young Readers
New York

pig

sty

frog

pond

eagle

nest

bee

hive

camel

desert

crab

tidal pool

beaver

dam

bear

cave

dog

doghouse

monkey

tree

hippopotamus

river

woodpecker

tree trunk

horse

stable

tiger

jungle

First published in the United States 1996 by
Dial Books for Young Readers
A Division of Penguin Books USA Inc.
375 Hudson Street
New York, New York 10014
Published in Great Britain 1996 by
Jonathan Cape, Random House
Copyright © 1996 by Christopher Wormell
All rights reserved
Printed in Hong Kong
First Edition
1 3 5 7 9 10 8 6 4 2

Library of Congress Catalog Card Number: 95-44730

The art for this book was created from handcut linoleum block
prints. Four blocks were cut for each picture. Each block was inked
with a roller and printed separately by hand, producing the black images
and the color areas. In certain instances, to achieve a shading or blending
of colors, more than one color ink was applied to the same block. All of
the art was color-separated by scanner and reproduced in full color.